Don't Let Go!

For Sophie, Joan and Geoff —J. W.

G. P. PUTNAM'S SONS,
a division of Penguin Putnam Books for Young Readers,
345 Hudson Street, New York, NY 10014.
G. P. Putnam's Sons, Reg. U.S. Pat. & Tm. Off.
First published in 2002 by Andersen Press, London.
Published simultaneously in Canada.
Printed in Italy. First American Edition, 2003.
Designed by Carolyn T. Fucile. Text set in Mrs. Eaves.
Library of Congress Cataloging-in-Publication Data
Willis, Jeanne. Don't let go! / Jeanne Willis ; illustrated by Tony Ross. p. cm.
Summary: Megan is nervous about her dad letting go of her bike as she learns to ride,
and her dad is nervous about how far into the world she will go once she does.
[1. Bicycles and bicycling—Fiction. 2. Growth—Fiction.
3. Fathers and daughters—Fiction. 4. Stories in rhyme.]
I. Ross, Tony, ill. II. Title. PZ8.3.W6799 Dp 2003 [E]—dc21
2002008537
ISBN 0-399-24008-X
1 3 5 7 9 10 8 6 4 2
First American Edition

Don't Let Go!

Jeanne Willis

Illustrated by Tony Ross

G. P. Putnam's Sons — New York

"Teach me to ride and I'll ride to you,
From Mom's house over to yours.

Please, will you, Daddy? I need to learn,
And Mom is too busy indoors.

"I tried in the yard, but it's really so hard;
I bloodied my knee on the wall.

At Grandma's house the road is too rough.
My wheels won't stay straight and I'll fall."

"Meg, there will always be slippery slopes
And ups and downs and bumps.
There will always be difficult paths to take
And giant steps and humps.

"But the view when you get to the top of the hill,
And the feel of the wind in your hair!
And the freedom to go wherever you please
And to know you can get yourself there . . .

"That must be worth a few little knocks
And maybe a bruise or two,
But if you're not ready, we'll wait a while—
Whatever you want to do."

"I'll try in a minute—at least, I might.
I'm getting myself prepared,

Checking my helmet and bicycle bell . . .
But, Daddy, I'm really scared."

"Megan, I'm here—
I won't let go,
Not until you say.

Hold on tight. I love you, so
We'll do this together, okay?"

"I think I'm ready
to go now, Dad.
Daddy, don't let go!
Don't . . .
Okay,
you can let go now!

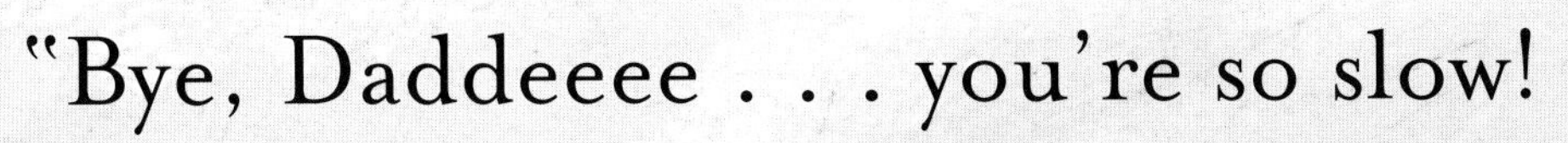

"Bye, Daddeeee . . . you're so slow!

"Look at me, Daddy! I can ride!
See? I can ride my bike.
Now I can go wherever I want,
To the end of the world if I like!"

"Megan, it's difficult letting go.
I was scared too today—

Scared you would never come back to me
Now that you can ride away."

"Daddy, I'm here. I won't let go,
Not until you say.
Hold on tight. I love you, so

We'll do this together, okay?"